Freedom to Choose

Sam LaRose

Published by Ink Stained Fingers Press, 2020.

FREEDOM TO CHOOSE

First edition. April 16, 2020.

ISBN: 979-8215285060

Written by Sam LaRose.

Author's Note & Content Warning

Freedom to Choose was originally written sometime between 2010 and 2012. I'm not 100% sure of an accurate date, due to the number of computers I've upgraded through over the years, which has altered my document create date (at least, on at this particular machine.) This is worth noting because...damn, I was *dumb* back then.

There are a few things that I've changed since originally releasing this as a free short story in 2020. First and foremost, I fixed a number of typos. I'm sure I missed some. Alas, it is the bane of all authors and publishers –traditional and independent. I used to have this really terrible habit of everything being very stream of conscious (much like this is). I also had some really annoying style choices, like people nodding at everything. That has probably been replaced with people *sighing* at everything. Can't win them all, I guess.

But the absolutely most deplorable thing that Past-Sam used to write is: unsafe sex practices and the Gay-For-You trope. If you read my other work, you'll notice that I very specifically mention safe sex practices, specifically condoms. In *Something More*, Kyle mentions gloves for anal fingering. In a (as of 3/2023) unreleased Mora Stephen's book, there is mention of dental dams. I believe very, very strongly that writing realistically about safe sex practices is essential.

As authors, we don't know who is going to read our books. If this were to fall into the hands of a naïve college (or even high school) student, who only read words waxing rhapsodic about how *good* it feels to raw dog inside another person... I'm nauseous just thinking about it, actually.

I'm not here to preach safe sex, I swear. But I will always strive to include it. To the point where I altered 1 of the 2 scenes in this book to include it. So, why didn't I also alter the first? Well...that's a complicated explanation. On one hand, I originally wrote this before I had this stringent mentality around showing proper condom use and (to an extent) technique. It felt disingenuous to past-me to not leave this as the story that Past-Sam apparently wanted to tell. And Present-Sam has grown up and is fairly rational. So, I'm going to leave it to be. At least in part.

If Present-Sam was writing this story, it would have been much different. And that's actually because I absolutely abhor a Gay For You story. I tweaked some language around here to make Patrick more self-aware of his attraction from the beginning. To try and explain *why* he wanted to stick with the Straight label instead of the Gay, Bi, Pan, or any other label. As I was reading through this, I also considered whether or not I had accidentally written a demiromantic character.

Gay For You is a harmful trope. Unfortunately, when I started reading Men-Loving-Men fiction –it was rampant. It still is, really. Between studies and anecdotal observation, it's a fairly common thought that men are more willing to hook up with other men (and trans folks) than women are. (Is this because of female internalized homophobia? Possibly. The number of Late In Life lesbians seems to be rising, with many awakenings being recorded and documented via social media like TikTok. Anyway –the trope!) Part of the reason that this trope became so engrained in MLM fiction is because...until the last few years, a LOT of MLM fiction was written by Cisgender Heterosexual Women.

There are a lot of conversations out on the internet about Cis-Het Women writing Gay romance. For a long time, I thought *I* was a cishet woman writing gay romance. After all, I have a vagina. I use she/her pronouns fairly often (because I live in a rural, conservative area where the argument is not worth my safety). While I have identified as pansexual for nearly a decade now, I didn't start identifying as non-binary until I was probably 28 or so. I wasn't public about it until I was 30. I'm part of the queer community. Does that give me a pass? No. It doesn't. But I recognize that men are different from women and do my absolute best to try and create characters who are true to life. A *lot* of cis-het women MLM authors are simply writing "women with dicks" (and I don't mean transwomen fiction, which honestly there should be more of!)

When it boils down to it: Gay For You is based on the premise that a man is 100% straight until he finds the fairy tale man of his dreams. Now, I know a LOT of gay men who love a good fairy tale and even a little magic –that is not how Gay For You works. At least one of the men is usually openly gay, or at least already questioning. The other is touted as very much straight. And essentially, it feels like the Gay Man has predatorily *turned* the straight man gay. Gay men have been calling this trope problematic for years, giving an unrealistic expectation to young gay men, who may put themselves in dangerous situations in order to fulfill the fantasy this trope has engrained in them.

The more and more you read these books, and the more critically you read them, the grosser the entire trope feels. I've been reading it since at *least* 2006 and been incredibly critical of it since about 2016.

I admit that I considered, after re-reading this work, completely pulling it from distribution. However, when it comes down to it: while this was an older work that could use some deep-dive TLC if I ever wanted to elaborate on this story and these characters to a full-length work, I do like this story just the way that it is. I think Patrick and Devin are both unique. Maybe some day I'll come back to this and give them an improved series of events and really get into their attitudes and behaviors. But for now, this work is what it is.

If you enjoy this work, I heartily encourage you to check out my full-length novels that make up the Dark Little Town trilogy and the spin-off Dylan Duology. I am also releasing the first of a new contemporary sports romance (as seen at the back of this edition) in May 2023. It may very well be one of the best things I've ever written. I think folks who read my work in order see my improvement over time as a writer.

Thanks for picking this up. I hope you enjoy it.

Content Warning: Profanity, unsafe sex practices, on-page sex acts, internalized homophobia, potentially problematic character interactions around sex acts.

Freedom to Choose

I was twelve years old when I ran into my mother's study and declared quite loudly to her: "Mom, I'm straight!"

She looked up from her computer, where she was most likely player Spider Solitaire and not writing. Like she was supposed to be doing. She looked a little surprised.

"Huh?"

"I just wanted you to know –I'm straight."

"...Okay?" She sounded confused.

"I'm not gay."

I could tell she was trying to hide her smile. I felt a flush of embarrassment move over my body. I realized the moment she leaned back in her chair and started laughing, that what I had declared was silly. Of *course* I was straight. Something like 70% of Americans were straight...10% were openly gay. The remaining 20% were confused, questioning, or in hiding. My blush crept up my cheeks. Mom turned in her chair to hold out her arms.

"Come here."

I moved around the desk and leaned into her. Her arms felt good as they wrapped around me. Sure, I was twelve and starting to get over my Mommy-complex. I still loved her hugs.

"Look," she finally said, leaning back again, "just because I write about gay men, doesn't mean that I want you to be one. If you are, that's fine. If you're not, that's OK too. I love you very much." She tilted her head, giving me a quizzical look. "Where'd this come from anyway?"

I looked down at my hands, suddenly fidgety.

"I was watching TV. They were making fun of you."

She rolled her eyes. "Screw them. This is because I finally sold the rights to one of my series and it got picked up for a movie. This will pass, sweetie. Don't let the media get to you. They may attack me, but I won't ever let anyone make assumptions about you." She pulled me down to kiss my forehead. "C'mon. Turn off the TV. You have homework you need to finish."

Fast forward eight years. I had no idea what I was doing in the hotel room with one of the actor's from one of my Mom's movies.

...Well, it wasn't really her movie. It was based on her book. The fourth film, based on her gay, semi-erotic novels.

My Mom had taught me that being gay or straight didn't matter, so long as I was OK with myself. When Josh had come on to me, it had been hard to resist. He was cute. I liked the way he always looked kind of scruffy, like he had just rolled out of bed.

"What's the matter?" His voice was as soft as his lips, kissing my neck.

I bit my tongue. I was twenty years old. Josh wasn't a whole lot older. I was straight. Or at least as straight as I could be, what with his hands being down my pants. He was openly gay and fit the bill of his character pretty damn well.

"You should probably know," I finally said, "...I don't usually do this kind of thing."

Josh grinned softly. "Your mom is like a queer goddess. You're telling me you don't have pretty boys coming on to you all the time?"

"I do. I don't usually give in to them."

He raised an eyebrow. "Oh really? Does that make me an exception?"

"Kind of."

He laughed, pulling me towards the bed with him. "Don't fret." He pushed me down into the mattress before straddling me underneath him. "Nothing's going to happen you don't want." He kissed me on the mouth. I found my arms moving of their own volition, wrapping around his neck. He hummed softly, his fingers coaxing under my shirt. After a few minutes he frowned, leaning back to look at me. "Is something wrong, Patrick?"

My eyes widened and I shook my head. "N-no. Why?"

"You don't seem that into it. We can stop if you don't want to do this."

"I-I'm sorry."

He sighed heavily before shifting off me. Comfortable on the bed, he leaned on his elbow, looking across at me instead. "Talk to me."

"Talk to you?"

"Yeah. Tell me what's going on up here." He reached over to tap my forehead. I reached up to rub the spot.

"Nothing. I told you, I don't really do this."

"You got a boyfriend or something?"

"I'm not gay."

He laughed. He had kind of a catty bark that made me want to wince. "If you're not gay, why'd you come up here with me? I thought I made it obvious what I wanted to do to you."

"Yeah, the 'fuck you right, but good' line was very clear." I turned my head to look at him. "I'm straight, Josh, but I'm not...*straight*."

"Bi?" He tried to label me. Like my years of introspection and self-awareness of my own attraction habits were more clear to him as an outsider.

"More like curious. Look at the books my mom's written. It piques my interest. It's something that has always been *normal*."

"But...you're not gay."

I shook my head. "No. I don't think so."

He nodded, shifting onto his back to stare up at the ceiling. When he didn't say anything, I bit my lip. I was kind of worried that I had offended him or something. But I was a big boy. I knew what I was doing. If I wasn't open to having sex with him, I wouldn't have come upstairs with him.

"I'm sorry, I'll go." I stood up. He leaned up on his elbows again, watching me pick up my jacket.

"Are you going to be on set tomorrow?"

I shook my head. "No. Mom wanted me to come down and make sure they weren't destroying her book. I'm going home tomorrow."

"Oh..."

I smiled, pulling on my jacket. It wasn't necessary, given the California heat, but the weight of it was comforting. "You seem sad about that."

"I am. I didn't get to go make good on my promise."

"Promise?"

"To fuck you but good."

I blushed, looking away and shaking my head. My keys jingled as I pulled them from my pocket. "Maybe next time."

"Is there going to be a next time?"

I shrugged. I didn't really have an answer for that because I genuinely didn't know. Acting as Mom's proxy was never planned very far in advance.

He got up from the bed, catching me by my belt loops as I was starting for the door. My back pressed against the door. The knob wedged uncomfortably in my back. It felt like he was devouring my mouth. His nails scraped my skin as he forced his hands up my shirt.

"What are you doing?" I asked when he finally came up for air.

"I can't let you leave if I don't know that you're coming back. Not without making sure I'll have you crawling back for more."

"That's a high order, isn't it?"

"It's the truth. No one can get enough of me if I hold onto them long enough." He kissed me roughly again, hugging me close. I shifted when I felt his pending hard-on against my thigh. He bit gently on my bottom lip, sucking it. Finally he looked up at me, his eyes big pools of sapphire blue. "I gotta know. Have you done it with other guys before?"

"Sure."

"Is that a 'yes' sure?"

"I have. A few different occasions."

He stepped away from me to lean on the side table behind him. "Good to know."

"...Are you done?" I asked. "Can I go home now?"

"You don't have to, but you can."

I couldn't help but smirk. "You're kind of a tease, aren't you?"

"Maybe a little."

I pushed my way between his knees. He almost knocked over the lamp as I flattened him onto the tabletop behind him. I tried to return his kiss as fiercely as he had done to me, but I wasn't sure I was succeeding. He groaned, pushing back. His hands were on my face, his thumbs stroking my cheeks.

"Fuck," he sighed. He panted, his tongue against his lip. "If you don't leave soon, I won't be able to let you go."

I ignored him and instead reached up to brush my fingers against the scruffy stubble on his face. "This whole five-o'clock shadow you've got going on is kind of sexy."

"Now who's the tease? Sayin' your straight but turning on all of the charm." He tsked, shaking his head. He pressed a quick kiss to my lips before wrapping his arms around my shoulders. "It's your call, Patrick. We can go back to the bedroom. Get naked. I'll fuck you like you've never been fucked in your life. ...Or you can go back your room and we won't see each other until the movie premier. If you choose the latter, I can guarantee you're going to spend the next year or so, wondering what could have happened."

"Yeah, but if I leave now, I can keep saying that I'm straight."

He grinned. "Would being something else be so bad?"

"Not if I hadn't kept insisting to my Mom that I was."

"I think she'd understand." It was like his hands were setting fire to my skin as he reached down. His fingers moved under the waistband of my jeans. He licked my lips before sucking at my throat.

"Ah, damn..." I sighed, "don't leave any marks."

"Why not?" He asked, pinching my butt. "I like marking the guys I sleep with. It's like a primal, territorial thing."

"I gotta see my mom tomorrow. I don't want to explain."

He grinned. "Your mom is awesome and everything, but you gotta cut those apron strings. Seriously..."

"I can't help it, she's all I've got."

I couldn't tell him that she was sick. I couldn't tell anyone. She had sworn me, and everyone else who knew, to secrecy. I wasn't sure how I was going to live without her, but I had to make sure that every tedious whim was satisfied while she was still with us. I wanted her to be happy before she died. That was why I had come out here to the set. I wanted to make sure it was great for her. For her legacy.

Josh led me into the bedroom again, discarding our clothes along the way.

"Damn." He stared appreciatively at my dick. "I know I just had it in my hands but seeing it and touching it are two totally different things." I blushed, not able to hide myself without looking like a kid. He grinned, pushing me back onto the bed. "I'm giving you a compliment, Patrick."

"Sorry."

"You're so cute when you blush." He reached up, pressing his finger against my lips. "Suck."

I took his finger into my mouth, sucking softly on the tip. He moaned, pressing his face into my neck. A few moments later, he was stroking his damp finger along my backside, pressing softly into me. I grunted, turning my face into his neck.

"You've done this before," he coaxed. "Why are you so shy?"

"I've never...you know, done it like this."

"Oh," he let out a little laugh. "I'm incredibly impatient. If you want me suck you off or something, I can do that too." He leaned in and let his lips brush my ear as he whispered. "Other boys tell me I'm good at it, but I'm not sure." He stroked me with his free hand as he thrust his finger deeper inside. My breath caught, mouth opening in a gasp. He took the opportunity to give me a very deep kiss, his tongue sparring with mine. When he moved away, he ran his tongue along my entire length.

"Stay right here," he requested. There was another chaste kiss to punctuate the request. "I'll be *right* back."

I raised an eyebrow as he slid away from me. He disappeared from the suite's bedroom and I heard the bathroom door jiggle. When he came back in, he had rolled on a condom and was slicking himself up with lube. The bottle he had in hand was tossed onto the bed beside me.

"How do you want to do this?" I liked how warm his mouth was as his lips touched my skin. His hands were warm too as they wrapped around me.

"What do you mean?"

"What position would you like me to fuck you in."

"Oh, uh..." There was more than one? Maybe I needed to actually *read* Mom's books?

"Roll over. I think missionary would be best." He nudged my hip. Josh seemed perfectly happy to take the reins. I was content enough to let him push me around.

I had slept with three guys my entire life. Once my senior year of high school with a guy who loved my Mom's books. The second, my freshman year of college, the first time I ever got drunk (again, another fan of Mom), and then a year ago...

"Keep your head here," Josh whispered. I felt him behind me. I bit my lip as he started to push inside of me. I lowered my forehead to the mattress. My eye squeezed closed and I tried to relax. My fingers tightened around fistfuls of the hotel's thin comforter. He didn't say anything as he pressed his lips to the back of my shoulder. He was totally in. His slick hand moved around to grab a hold of me. The only thing I could muster out of my throat was some kind of guttural noise. I dipped forward involuntarily as he started to stroke me.

"Feel good?" He asked, his lips peppering my back. I moaned in reply as he pulled his hand away, grabbing a hold of my hips. "Ready?"

"Uh huh."

He didn't hold anything back. There was no slow progression like the other guys I had had sex with. He didn't care that I was a novice. I was quickly aware that he was just using me to get off. Scarily enough though, I couldn't begin to care... The slick sucking and squelching sounds of him violating me were enough to get everything else out of my head. It was just the two of us, in that spacious suite. Him fucking me, like if he stopped I was going to bolt. Me, trying so hard to take all of it in stride and enjoy it for what it was. Sex. No strings. No explanations.

"Fuck, fuck..." I turned my cheek against the mattress, reaching down between my legs to stroke myself. I listened to his own throaty moans. Between the fullness of his cock inside me, and his pleasure noises, I came in my hand just before his strokes began to slow, and his hip thrusts began to become less frantic and more relaxed.

"I love your ass," Josh sighed. It took him a second before he rolled away. I stretched my back, before sitting up to grab a tissue from the side table to wipe my hands off. I couldn't help but watch as he pulled off the condom, and tossed it into the trashcan next to the bed. "Where'd you learn to do that?"

"Learn to do what?"

He grinned, turning to look at me, "You're so cute when you act innocent." He turned onto his side to kiss me. "You're a little slut, aren't you? Telling me you're straight when you can take a fuck like that." He tsked, shaking his head. "I call your lies."

I licked my lips, shaking my head as I got up. "I should go."

He narrowed his eyes. "Patrick, wait..." I had already pulled on most of my clothes by the time he joined me in picking up my clothes. "What did I say?"

"You didn't say anything. I have an early flight tomorrow. I should go back to my room."

It took him a second but he nodded, "Right. When will I see you again?"

I shrugged. "I don't know. Depends on what my mom needs me to do for her."

He sat down on the edge of the bed, trying to hide his expression behind his hand. He watched me pull my jacket back on for the second time. I disappeared into the bathroom to wash my hands and make sure that I didn't have any visible indications of what had just happened on my clothes. I looked OK, I thought, as I exited the bathroom. Josh was getting dressed again too as I picked up my keys from where they had fallen on the floor when we'd resumed.

"Call me," he requested, grabbing the collar of my jacket. "The next time you're going to be in town. I took the liberty of putting my number on your phone. You should probably have a lock code, you know." He shoved my cell phone into my back pocket. "Maybe we can discuss this...trauma you have."

"I don't have a trauma." My lips quirked in smirk.

"If you didn't, you'd still be in bed with me." He kissed me one last time. "I'll see you."

"See you."

It was a little over a year before that I met Devin in the campus bookstore. Mom had just been diagnosed. I was looking for an outlet to get away from everything. She was in her anger stage and I didn't want to be the person she took everything out on, so I was distancing myself from her. When she was ready to move on, she knew how to get a hold of me. I was choosing to lay low and stay in school.

I wasn't really looking for anything, but I found myself in the midst of the bookstore's fiction section, staring at my Mom's earlier works. I recognized them from the shelf at home where she had them all lined up. I'd be the first to admit that I had never read one of her novels. I'd grown up in a fatherless home where she had worked herself nearly to death on her books all about the gay romance...but I'd never been inclined to pick one up. It gave me the creeps really, to even think about what went on in my Mom's head.

"This one is my favorite." A masculine hand tugged one of the titles an inch forward. "It's an earlier one of her works. Her new stuff is best, but the end makes me cry every time I read it."

I turned to look at him. It was obvious he didn't know who I was. A lot of her fanatical fans were just as obsessed with me as they were with Mom.

"Have you read it?" He raised an eyebrow.

"I've never read any of her books. As a matter of principle, I refuse to actually."

"Oh? You're missing out on some great literature. It's amazing that her books made it so mainstream. Probably because she's a woman." He followed me as I moved on along the shelf towards something a little safer. "Let me guess, you're a movie fan."

I shook my head. "I don't watch the movies either."

"Why not give it a try? You think she doesn't understand what it's like to be a queer in modern times? She's good," he assured me. "It's amazing how often she gets it right on the nose. Like she's writing, just for me."

I turned to look at him. He was cute, I would give him that. His dark hair was shaggy, and he was clean shaven. If it weren't for conversation, I wouldn't have immediately assumed he was gay. Not that I believed you could immediately tell a person's sexuality just by looking at them.

"You don't know who I am, do you?"

He squinted his eyes at me. "Hmm...should I?"

"No, of course not. Excuse me."

I brushed past him, but he caught my arm. As I turned back to protest, a camera flash went off in my face.

He wiggled the cell phone at me. "Alright, I'll find out who you are. I can assume I was a total ass and I'll need to apologize. How about giving me your phone number so I can say I'm sorry when the time comes?"

"I'm not gay," I declared, brushing him off.

"Never said you were." He held out his phone to me.

Against my better judgment, I took the phone and sent myself a text.

"I'll call you in a couple days. It'll probably take me that long to figure it out, I'm sure."

I didn't answer, handing him back his device. He watched me with curious interest as I walked away. I couldn't help but pause as I passed the window outside on my way to my next haunt. He was still watching me and gave me a little wave. I felt the blush creep up my face before I scurried away as quickly as I could without looking suspicious.

It was only a couple of hours before he called me.

"I am *such* an asshole," he announced when I answered. "Why didn't you just SAY you were Samantha Corner's son?"

"You didn't really give me the opening." I leaned back in my chair at my desk. I was back in my dorm room after dinner. I had a girl between my knees. She had looked up curiously when I had answered the phone.

"Still. I am a *total* asshole. I mean, going on about your mom's books! You must get come-ons like that all the time."

"It's alright." I put my hand on top of the girl's head, stroking her hair. "Look, I'm kind of busy right now. Can you call back later if you really feel the need to continue this discussion?"

"Oh, yeah. Of course." There was a pause. "...Is there a better time?"

"Give me fifteen minutes."

"Alright. I'll talk to you then."

After I hung up, I tossed my phone back onto the table. I let the girl finish me off without either of us mentioning the interruption. I felt bad that I didn't exactly remember her name. She lived down the hall and, like all the others, was a fan of my mom.

"Should I come back later?" She asked as I was subtly pushing her towards the door. "Maybe you'd like a little more than a blow job next time?"

I smirked. "Thanks for the offer. I'll get back to you." I managed to push her out into the hallway and to close the door before she could try and wedge her way back in. I sat back down in my chair, as the phone rang. Almost as if on cue.

"I want to take you out." There wasn't even a hello from him.

"I already told you I'm not gay."

"Again, I never said that you were. I said I want to take you out. For dinner. To apologize for being an idiot."

"That's not necessary. It happens more than you think."

"It doesn't happen to me. Please, let me take you out tonight."

"Why don't you start by telling me your name?" I countered. Perhaps ironic given the situation with the girl that I'd just kicked out.

"Ah fuck! I am an idiot! I'm sorry." His flustering made me smile. "I'm Devin Jonas. I'm a creative writing major."

"Well, Devin Jonas, I'm not interested."

"I'm not asking you out on a *date*, Patrick Corner," he chided. "I'm asking you out for an *apology dinner*."

"You know what would be better than a dinner?" I asked.

"...Is this something naughty?" He asked. His tone make me think that while he wanted to sound a bit aghast, he was up for that if it was what I wanted.

"What makes you ask that?"

"I detect this note in your voice that tells me you're going to ask me to come over and do something dirty with you. Am I wrong?" Yep, he was definitely on board.

"Very," I answered dryly. "I'm a visual arts major…I'd like to paint you for my human form class. I don't have many friends and I think this project would be best if I did it with a stranger anyway."

"Of course!" He sounded excited. "Is that okay though?"

"Yeah, it would be a really big help. There's one stipulation."

"Okay?"

"It's a nude portrait. You don't have to be totally nude. I don't have to see everything, but…you know. A lot of uncovered skin."

"Okay." The excitement wasn't disappearing. "I'd love to do it. Where and when do you want me?"

"Are you free tonight? I'd like to get started. I've been putting it off."

"Of course."

"Alright, I live in Putnam Hall, three-fourteen. We can do it in my room. Seven o'clock, okay?"

There was a pause while I assumed he wrote the information down. "I look forward to it."

"I'll see you then. Thanks for your help."

At six thirty, I set up my easel in front of the couch and started arranging my paints. I was just checking my brushes when there was a brief knock on the door.

I opened the door to Devin. He looked as cute as he had in the bookstore earlier that day. He was sporting a five o'clock shadow now, but it looked good on him. I tried not to let my eyes trail down and mentally undress him. I was going to see at least most of him actually undressed soon enough.

"Hey," I stepped back to usher him in, "thanks for doing this. I know it's a big ask."

"Not a problem." He started shrugging out of his jacket. "Where do you want me?"

"On the couch would be fine." I went to my desk, pulling out my trusty sketching pencils. "You can take off your clothes and put them on the desk. There's a blanket there if you want to cover up.

"Why would I want to do that?" He asked. I heard a rustle of clothes as he stripped. "It's not like you're the first guy to see me naked."

"I wasn't making any assumptions." I pulled my stool behind the canvas, looking out over the scene I'd created. He made himself comfortable on the couch. He'd man-sprawled in the middle of it and folded his hands behind his head.

"How's this?"

"Your arms are going to get tired. Make sure you're comfortable," I warned.

He chuckled, but moved. He scooted to one end of the couch, leaning against the arm instead and pulling his feet up onto the couch. I tilted my head. I liked the way the light was reflecting, but his features weren't standing out enough for me. "Do you mind a little make-up?"

"Make-up?" He repeated

I nodded, getting up to open my cosmetics drawer. I didn't wear make-up regularly, but I liked to keep a few things on hand for artistic reasons. "Not too much, I promise."

"C'mon, I'm gay. I don't mind a little make up." He rolled his eyes before watching me pull out some things from the drawer. I tried not to look down, away from his face, as I approached him with the eyeliner and lipstick.

"Close your eyes," I requested. I knelt by the corner of the couch. I couldn't help but touch his face. The pencil was smooth gliding as I traced his eyelids. "Okay, you can open them." I noticed he had very pale, hazel-colored eyes. They were eerily enhanced with the dark eyeliner. I didn't say anything as I rubbed the lipstick on my thumb before brushing it across his bottom lip. "This might hurt— "I pinched his mouth and he groaned.

"Ow –what was that for?"

"Color." I shrugged. I rubbed my thumb against his lips some more, tilting my head to look at his face. There was still something missing. I got up again and grabbed a can of hairspray.

"Hey, whoa..." He stopped me before I could even uncap it. "What the hell?"

"I don't like your hair. It's too flat."

"Flat?"

"Yeah, I want it...up." I took my hands away from him and sprayed his head liberally before pulling my fingers through it. I twisted a few locks of it between my fingers before I stepped back. It was better. Maybe not the best, but it was good enough given what I had on hand. I put the make-up and the hairspray away before wiping the lipstick off my hand with a towel.

"Are you always cold to your models?" He asked.

"Would you mind not talking? I'm starting now." I picked out a sharp pencil and began rough out the image. "You can talk once I finish the preliminary sketch."

He held in a sigh, relaxing back into position. I tried not to take notice of how he was purposely spreading his thighs. He bent his knee against the back of the couch. One hand rested on top of it, the other leaned on the arm, propping up his chin. As

I did the rough sketch, I was purposely ignoring his 'equipment'. After a half-hour or so, it was pretty hard to find other ways to occupy myself, so I just gave in and looked. I was very surprised to find that he was uncut. Not surprising was his lack of pubic hair. Like the other guys I had come into contact with, he most likely shaved. I wasn't sure why, but I had always had a severe distaste for baldness 'down here'. Even on the girls I had slept with. Unkempt was off putting too, but being completely barren of hair was immature and unnatural...but I kept it to myself as I sketched.

"How's it coming?"

"Just give me a few more minutes," I insisted. "Then you can talk all you want."

He sighed, turning his head to look out of the partly opened blinds. My room overlooked a barren lot, so I wasn't too concerned about anyone looking in my window. I looked at him for a moment, my pencil stopping midline. The pencil dropped from my hand immediately and I leaned over to grab my digital camera from the bookshelf. Luckily, he didn't turn until after the flash had gone off.

"What are you doing?"

"Stop moving. Turn back to the window," I shook my head. I fiddled with my settings as he hesitantly turned back. "Goddamn, that's perfect... I'm sorry—It was only your face. I'll show you later." I put the camera down, sitting back down with my pencils again. I averted my eyes from him as I finished the sketch. "Okay, you can move around a bit now if you want. I've got the basic sketch."

"Good," he sighed, stretching his arms above his head. "Man, staying still is harder than it sounds."

I didn't really answer as I started to uncap paints, mixing colors on my trusty paper plate.

"You didn't answer me before. Are you always so cold to your models?"

"I'm not being cold," I countered. "Trust me, if I were being cold to you, you would know."

"Oh, I dunno. It feels pretty chilly to me."

"I can tell." I couldn't stop the smile that tugged at my lips. He dropped his mouth open before looking down.

"Goddammit, I am not small!" He retorted. "In fact, this is kind of turning me on. You're teasing me." He looked up and caught my smile. "I see that little smirk on your face."

"I'm painting," I retorted.

He hummed, tilting his head to the side. "So...tell me about you."

"About me?" I raised an eyebrow. "There isn't a whole lot to tell that isn't readily available on the internet."

"I want to hear it from you." He pouted, sticking out his bottom lip. I was overcome by the urge to get up and suck on it. I shook my head briefly, trying to focus back on the canvas. "C'mon...tell me what it was like growing up with the total goddess that is Samantha Corner."

"She's a mom. There's not that much to say."

"What's she like?" He insisted.

"She's nice," I answered, "but she annoys the hell out of me. As most moms do their kids. She's got a Peter Pan complex and makes me feel like I have the adult while she's the kid sometimes."

"You take care of her?"

"It can feel like that. She knows when she needs to be my mother and grow up. She writes a lot, and that makes her solitary. You wouldn't believe how much unpublished stuff she has just lying around. Her office is filled with notebooks. Her desk is littered with disks. She's got about four external hard drives." I glanced up at him. "Writing is her life. What she lives to do. What she was meant to do. She's not so great at the human interaction, even with me. She has a habit of making me feel like I was an accident. An inconvinence. Even though she never means to."

"That's kind of harsh, isn't it?"

"I said she doesn't mean to," I countered. "I know that she loves me, and probably couldn't live without me. That doesn't change that since I was old enough to take care of myself, she's had a habit of pushing me to a second priority to her deadlines."

"She doesn't sound like a very nice person," Devin decided.

"She can be a shit mother, but she's a wonderful, passionate person. I wouldn't trade her for anyone."

He nodded, scratching his chest. I noticed how smooth he was in general. I couldn't help but ask.

"Why do you shave?"

"Excuse me?"

"You're totally hairless, aside from your head. Why do you shave?"

"That's a personal question, isn't it?"

"You've already psychoanalyzed my relationship with my mother. I figured it was a fair question."

"I shave because my boyfriend liked it."

"Lik*ed* it?" I emphasized the past tense.

"Yeah," he nodded, "we just broke up."

"How long did you date for?"

"Two years," he replied easily. "He cheated on me with some guy on the cheerleading squad. How junior high is that?"

"Maybe you just weren't flexible enough for him?" I suggested.

"I'm plenty flexible. He wasn't versatile enough. I ask him to fuck me just one time, and he gets all nervous." He rolled his eyes. "I'm better off without him anyway."

"Well, you don't seem bitter at all," I assured him.

"Cocky bastard." He looked back at me. "As long as we're getting into it, I have to know. You ever sleep with a guy before? Or are you as straight as you want everyone to think you are?"

"I'm straight," I answered, "but that doesn't mean I haven't slept with guys before."

"Oh really?" He asked, raising an eyebrow.

"Yeah, really."

"Tell me more," he requested.

"I'd rather not. I hardly know you. How do I know you wouldn't just stick it up on the internet somewhere? Outing Samantha Corner's son."

"Why would I do something like that? I love your mom. That'd piss her off, right?"

"My Mom knows I'm straight."

"Does she know you've slept with boys?" His tone turned amused.

"I don't tell my mom about my sex life." I tried to focus more on my brush strokes and less on the conversation. "Chances are, she'd become too interested and use me for information. You might not know this, but she can't talk to gay guys. They make her nervous."

"Why?" He laughed.

"Part of it is because she doesn't want to know what they think of her books. She's afraid of being very wrong or even very right. The other part of it is that Mom is very shy."

"That's got to be kind of tough."

"She has all her fan letters screened. She doesn't reply personally. She doesn't do book signings. She lives rather sheltered life."

"That's kind of depressing."

"It's just the way she works."

We were quiet for a bit before he yawned. "So, how's the painting coming?"

"Fine. Do you mind if a take a couple of whole body shots, so I can keep working on it tomorrow morning? You can cover up if you'd rather I didn't have a dick pick."

He laughed. "Wouldn't be the first guy with one. Go right on ahead. –I wasn't mad about the pic earlier. Just startled."

"Thanks." I took the moment to rinse out my brush and take a quick picture with my camera. I hoped the light wouldn't shift too much while I worked.

We were quiet for a little longer. I had been painting for about two hours when I noticed his eyelids were starting to get a little heavy.

"I'm sorry." I stood up, stretching my arms. "Do you want to take a break? This can't be very exciting for you."

"I'm okay," he insisted.

"Do you want something to drink?"

"A water would be great."

I pulled out two bottles of water from the mini fridge and tossed one in his direction.

"Do you have a roommate?" He nodded towards the bunked beds, both of which were made. "I see you all over this room, but no evidence of another person."

"I don't," I admitted. "I like to keep the other bed made because keeping it bare looks tacky. Plus, you never know when someone will need a place to crash."

"Someone?" He raised an eyebrow.

"I have *some* friends. Honest."

"Okay, I get it." He yawned, stretching his arms out. I tried not to watch the way his muscles contracted when he made the movement. I couldn't help it. He looked good, and it had been a long time since I had gotten more than a blow job.

He caught me looking a grin crossed his face. He wasn't shy at all about running his hand down his chest to his crotch. "You like what you see, Straight Boy?"

"It's not bad," I replied, taking a plug from my ice-cold water. The chill reminded me that this painting was due in two days. I needed to get better get control of my hormones. I couldn't help but tease him a little. "I'd like it more if you didn't look prepubescent."

"Oooh, that hurts." He cringed before looking straight back at me. "I just broke up with the guy that liked it a few days ago. It'll grow back. ...I kind of like it smooth." He was teasing me now, his fingers trailing his balls. "It's so easy to touch."

"Each to their own, I suppose."

"You can touch it, if you want," he offered. "I don't mind."

"I have a painting to finish. I'd like if it you didn't get too excited."

"Are you sure? Maybe taking a little sex break would help. You look so tense behind the canvas. Is it not going well?"

"It's going fine. I'm just on a deadline."

"Fucking me might help relieve some stress."

"You want me to fuck you?" I raised an eyebrow.

"My ex was a hardcore bottom." He stood up, stretching his arms above his head. "I tried to get him to take me a couple of times, but he wigged out. It's been a long time since I've gotten a real cock in my ass." He came closer, ignoring the canvas to press close to me. I was *extremely* aware of how naked he was. My awareness became his awareness when he grabbed hold of me through my jeans, stroking me with his V'd fingers.

"You sure you're as straight as you say you are?"

"I'm straight. I'm not dead."

He leaned forward and kissed me. I thought I might die. A guy had never had that kind of effect on me before. Come to think of it, a girl hadn't either. But he was different. I just wanted to touch him. I wanted to pull him close and do anything he wanted. I was flooded with the overwhelming urge to fuck him until he cried for mercy. To kiss him until he could barely breath.

"Not bad," he decided when we finally parted.

"I've been around the block a couple of times when it comes to kissing."

"You've been guys before. Top or bottom? Most straight guys are tops, but you don't strike me as the top-type."

"I've done both," I admitted.

"And which do you prefer?"

"Women." ...Except apparently for *him*. For whatever mystical reason, Devin Jonas was an exception to the rule. I hated what my mother might think if I'd told her I had had an honest-to-god *gay for you* moment.

"C'mon," he didn't even look down as he started undoing my belt, "you like me. You wouldn't be so hard if you didn't find me attractive."

"Attractive yes," I acknowledged. "I can control myself though."

"Can you?" He raised an eyebrow. "If you could really control yourself, wouldn't I be back on that couch, with all that space between us?"

He had a point.

"Okay, so I don't have *that* much control. I still haven't just flipped you over the stool and fucked you senseless yet. I'm ahead in that sense." I managed to get his hands out of my pants, and to push him back towards the couch. "Go sit down, so I can continue with my painting, huh?"

He didn't put up a fight and sat back down. Just as he had been for the previous two and half hours, with his leg bent and display his half-hard cock. We didn't say much for another hour or so. It was starting to get late. I was having a harder time concentrating on painting instead of my model.

"I think that's enough." I stood, kicking my stool towards the closet and turned my easel towards the wall.

"Can I see it so far?" He asked, getting up to start pulling on his clothes. I tried not to let the wash of disappointment bother me. It was better that he was dressing and making his way out quickly. It was nearly midnight and I didn't know how far he had to walk back to his own dorm.

"When it's done, I'll let you see it. I've barely started."

He frowned. "Aw, c'mon..."

"Are you a free again tomorrow night?" I asked. "I can work from the picture during the day, but I'd like to keep the flesh-and-blood display for at least another night. I can probably finish it tomorrow if I work on it all day."

"Don't you have classes?"

"I do." I shrugged.

He nodded, pulling his jeans up over his hips. "Tomorrow night, are you going to be less of a jackass when I come on to you?"

"Probably not."

He sighed. "Then I'll just have to try harder." He put his hands against my face to kiss me again. His tongue probed into my mouth. I tried not to let it surprise me. He was smiling as he backed away. "I'll see you same time tomorrow?"

"I'll be here."

"I look forward to it then, Patrick Corner." He patted my cheek before showing himself out of my dormitory.

The next day, I made sure that I was prepared for Devin's arrival. I had worked feverishly on the painting all day. I still managed to acquaint my cock with my right hand at least twice before he arrived at seven. I was just packing myself away when he knocked on the door.

"Hey, come in." I had turned the canvas towards the wall so he couldn't see it. I had tried not to touch the couch or lamp that I had been using for lighting. "Could you just stand there for a minute? I need to do your eyes and lips again."

He closed the door behind him and waited patiently while I pulled out the eyeliner and lipstick from the night before. I tried to ignore how good his skin felt under my fingers when I brushed my thumb over his lips. I stepped away from him to wipe my hand on a spare towel again. My room was littered with empty paint tubes, paper plates covered in paint residue, and empty water bottles.

"Sorry about the mess. I don't clean much when I'm working to finish a project."

"It's okay. I hardly noticed it," he lied. Devin moved towards the couch, taking off his shirt. I turned the canvas back to its place and pulled my brushes out again. When he was naked, he sat on the couch, resuming his pose from the night before. I put some fresh paint on my plate.

"You can turn on the TV or radio if you want. We don't have to sit in such silence."

"Ah, but Patrick, your silence speaks volumes about you," he teased. "Plus, it's cute to watch how frustrated you get."

"I don't get frustrated," I retorted.

"Yes, you do," he insisted. He reached over to pick up the remote, flipping on the TV.

I kept working at a more precise pace then I had kept during the day. By eleven o'clock, Devin had shifted and wasn't really posing anymore. It was OK because I was nearly done. Just putting in final touches. His eyes were closed, and I was pretty sure he was asleep. I stepped back from the painting completely at midnight. I decided if it wasn't finished, it wasn't ever going to be. Devin's head had lolled to the side, and he was breathing softly. He had tugged a blanket over his waist. I hated to wake him when he looked so peaceful. Instead, I let him be.

I turned off the lights and TV. I stripped down to my boxers in the dark before climbing into bed. I had an eight A.M. class in the morning that I couldn't skip, no matter how much I wanted to. I turned against the wall, pressing my forehead against the cool brick.

I wasn't asleep for long when I felt warm arms wrapping around me. At first, I was a little startled, but then realized it could only be one person.

"I have a top bunk for a reason, Devin."

"I always hated sleeping on the top bunk." He nipped at my ear. "I had a tendency of falling out."

"Then I'll sleep up top and you can sleep down here. It doesn't make a difference to me."

"Or we could stay right where we are." He leaned over me, turning my face towards his so he could kiss me. I could taste the lipstick that still stained his lips. "C'mon, Patrick. It's just for a couple of hours."

"I don't want to have sex with you right now." I turned back to the wall, pressing my arm over my face.

"I never said you had to," Devin admonished. "I just want to share a bed with you. It's too late to walk back to my dorm. It's not safe, you know?" He tried to nudge my arm away from my face and pouted when he wasn't successful. "Aw, c'mon..."

"You can stay here, I don't care. But if you're staying in this bed, it's purely platonic."

His arms wrapped around me and he gave a more contented sigh, pressing his face against my shoulder. "Hmm, you feel good."

I squeezed my eyes closed and tried to ignore him. He had gotten half dressed, which I was thankful for... At the same time, I was a little disappointed. I couldn't squelch this feeling of wanting to take him in my hands, in my mouth, and make him moan. I was pretty sure he had a great sounding moan.

"You're getting excited." His fingertips brushed over my crotch. "I can feel it. Your back is all tense too."

"A warm body is a body; it doesn't matter what kind of equipment is attached to it."

Devin was quiet for a moment. His fingers stroked a featherlight trail down my side that made me want to shiver.

"Why is it so important for you not to be gay, Patrick?"

"It's not. It's tiresome that people make comments that my mom made me gay just because of the kinds of books she writes. So...I'm straight. Not to mention that I like women more than I like men."

"I can understand that, I guess," he conceded. "That must be frustrating. I'll stop teasing you." He rolled away from me, taking up the rest of the bed as he spread out, stretching. "Goodnight, Patrick."

"Goodnight, Devin."

After that, it's weird to say, but we started dating. I kept telling him that our "dates' were just two friends, hanging out, but he loved to see my blush when he introduced me to his friends as his boyfriend.

"I'm not his boyfriend," I would correct. "I'm straight." His friends would laugh at that, like it was a joke. After awhile, I started to feel like it was a joke too. My whole sexuality was a sham. Devin would get jealous if I looked at girls. He'd hold my hand or even kiss me in public to make sure that everyone knew that he had dibs on me. Like I was a piece of prime choice meat. But I didn't stop him either. I held his hand because I liked how soft his skin was. I kissed him because the taste of his mouth, usually citrusy thanks to his love of lemon drops, was totally sweet and intoxicating. I also didn't mind so much when he spent the night, refusing the couch or the top bunk so he could feel me up.

But we weren't having sex.

And we kept not having sex for almost three months. It was Devin that snapped. He had cuddled against my chest as we watched a Made-for-TV movie on one of those channels that specialized in Made-for-TV movies. He started kissing me, which was fine. He started stroking his fingers down my chest, which was fine too. But when he started to unfasten my jeans...that wasn't fine.

"Hey, c'mon..." I pulled his hands away. "We're watching a movie."

"All we ever do is watch movies. I want you—no, I need you to fuck me." He gave me what I supposed he wanted to be a savage kind of kiss. "What do you say? Get hot and dirty with me."

I shook my head, conflicted. "Devin, don't be like this."

"You're my boyfriend! I want to have sex with you, Patrick! What's wrong with that?"

"I am not your boyfriend," I replied evenly.

"Then what are we, huh? I think about you every second we're not together. We go out on dates. We sleep in the same bed. We make out like crazy." He pressed his forehead to mine, staring into my eyes. "What am I to you?"

"I don't know," I answered, trying not to get sucked in by his gaze. "I try not to put tags on everything."

"Patrick," he groaned, pushing closer. I could feel him, pressing against my thigh. I hoped he couldn't tell I was just as turned on by our close contact as he was. "Please! If it doesn't go well, or you truly don't like it, I'll give up. I'll stop trying. We'll just be friends."

"Why do you want to have sex with me so badly?"

"Why wouldn't I?"

"I can think of lots of reasons."

He sighed, tugging his fingers through my hair. He gave me a couple of peck-like kisses before he gave me his best pout. "I know hearing this is going to make you uncomfortbale, but…I think I love you."

"You can't love me," I said. "You barely know me."

"I know how you make me feel. When you're not pushing me away and being and ass…" He sighed. "I *know* I love you."

"Devin, stop it." I pushed him away so I could get up from the couch.

"Does it bother you because I can say it out loud? Or because you feel the same way?"

"Devin…" It was cliché, but I had this inner-turmoil thing going on. I wanted so badly to give in to him, to tell him that I loved him too… But, I couldn't maintain my straight identity if I had a boyfriend.

I guess being straight wasn't a big deal. I'd never been a fan of tags, but since I realized what my mother's profession entailed, I always felt like I had to keep up this wall that clearly stated who I was. Devin made me rethink that wall.

"C'mon." He was kneeling on the couch, his hands folded neatly in his lap. I could tell he wanted to reach out to me. Touch me. I wanted him to touch me, but if he did, I was more than sure I couldn't say no to him anymore. "You have to open up to me. You don't have to be all manly for me. You're not going to scare me away by being honest with me about your emotions."

I blew out a hard breath, turning away from him. I heard him get up, and he wrapped his arms around me from behind. I closed my eyes when I felt his cheek against my back.

"I know this hard for you. You've spent your whole life trying to be straight for reasons I only half understand. But, it's okay. A lot of 'straight' guys aren't as straight as they think they are."

"It's not like that. I don't have a problem being with men."

"Then what's wrong?"

"I don't know," I shrugged. "Part of me really wants to give in to you, I'll admit it. But there's still that part that says if I do have sex with you, I can't say I'm straight anymore."

"You've slept with guys before. You've told me that. Why am I different?"

"Because I care about you," I admitted. "If I have sex with you, I can't deny being your boyfriend. The other guys...they were stupid mistakes. They used me to fulfill some kind of a fantasy. To get closer to my mom. To her characters. I can't do that with you."

"I like *you*, Patrick. I want to be *your* boyfriend. Your mom has nothing to do with it."

"You say that now. What about after we have sex?"

"What about it?"

"What if we have sex and it's not any good?"

"Babe. Any sex is good sex," he laughed. He turned me around to kiss me. "If it's not up to par, I'll teach you. I'll turn you in a certified sex machine."

"Devin..."

"Patrick."

"I can't just *have sex* with you."

"Why not?" He asked. "I'm ready. You're ready." He started unbuttoning his jeans. "All we have to do is get naked."

"I don't have, you know, stuff."

"Stuff?" He raised an eyebrow.

"You know. Condoms. Lube." I went along with him as he pulled my t-shirt over my head.

He rolled his eyes. "Alright, so condoms are probably a sensible thing given the times we live in –but I promise, I am totally DDF. If you want me too, I can walk to my dorm and get you my last screen report. It's only a like two months old and I haven't seen anyone but you since."

"I doubt that's necessary."

"As for lube...we can make do. Spit works just as a well. Or cum." His lips brushed my bare shoulder. I found my fingers inching under the back of his shirt. It wasn't long before I had pulled it over his head and tossed it to the floor by my own.

"Or we could just go to the gas station down the street and pick some up," I suggested.

"Yeah, if you want to stall," he snorted.

"Look, I haven't slept with a guy in...a while." I stopped him from pushing my jeans and boxers down.

"Good." He wrapped his arms around my neck, leaving my pants alone. "Forget everything you ever did with those fools. I want a fresh slate. A real virgin to the art. I want to blow your mind." He pushed me back onto the bed. He grabbed the bottom of my jeans and yanked. Hard. I groaned as they were essentially torn from my body and tossed to the floor. He pushed off his own before he got on top of me, seeking out my mouth again with his.

"Uhh—Devin..."

"Trust me a little, okay? You don't have to do anything. Just, you know, lay there." He straddled my hips.

I did as he asked, word for word, to the best of my ability. It didn't take very long until he was impaling himself on me for the first time. He was on top, his hands gripping tightly on my shoulders. I was totally enthralled with the way that his body moved. Even when I had sex with women, I had never paid much attention to anything other than the fact that I was getting some.

"Tell me when you're going to cum," he requested. He took my hand and put it against his stomach. I was mesmerized by the feel of his abdominal muscles tightening and flexing as he thrust over me. His fingers stroked down my chest, and he leaned forward to press a quick kiss to my lips. "You're kinda quiet..."

"I'm soaking it all in."

He hummed as I wrapped my hand around his member, jerking him off. He had to have felt ignored. The only action his cock had been getting was the methodical slap against my abs. But he was hard as a rock and dripping pre-come, regardless.

"Are you close?" He asked, nuzzling my neck. He groaned as he stretched forward.

"If it...if it hurts, you don't have to keep going."

"I like it," he assured me. "I'm just running a little dry is all..." He kissed me again, swirling his tongue around mine. His mouth opened wide, and he gasped, "*Ah, fuck*..." He tightened up as he emptied in spurts onto my abs. The sight of him was enough to set me off too. I barely had enough time to warn him and slip out. After I had unloaded on his backside, he pushed me back inside. He rocked forward, kissing me. When he finally slid to my side and laid his head against my chest, his breathing was starting to return to normal.

I wrapped an arm around his waist and pressed my chin to the top of his head. He looked up, and I noticed little worry lines across his forehead and at the corners of his eyes.

"What?" I brushed my fingertips over his hair.

"Are...was I okay?"

I smiled, kissing his forehead. "Yeah, but uh...we've definitely got to stock up on the condoms and lube before we do that again."

After that, we had sex all the time. He basically lived in my room with me. He woke me up with blow jobs in the morning. We met periodically between our classes for quickies against the door. At night we fought for position, except it wasn't much of a fight since he typically let me win. After another three months of finally giving in to him... It was over.

"What's wrong?" He caught my arm as I was frantically packing a bag. "What's going on?"

"Family emergency." I shrugged off his arm to keep packing.

"Your mom? What happened? Is she okay?"

"I can't really talk about it."

"Can I come with? Maybe I can help."

"Devin." I stopped. I took his face between my palms and kissed him as hard as I could. "I can't do this right now."

"Okay." His voice was breathy and worried. "When are you coming back?"

"I don't know."

"Patrick..." He put his hands on my wrists. "It'll be okay. Relax."

"Devin, no, you don't understand. I can't—I might not be coming back."

"What do you mean? We still have like two months of school left."

"I know."

"What is going on?"

"I'm really sorry."

"Sorry for what? I don't understand. I came over to see if you wanted lunch."

I took a deep breath. "Devin, I can't see you anymore."

His eyes narrowed in confusion and hurt. I knew those five words had been a direct stab to the heart. They were doing a number on me too. Between what was possibly waiting for me at home and what was happening there in my dorm, I was overwhelmed. The pressure of tears building behind my eyes and the tenseness in my shoulders, as well as the echoing words of Mom's assistant telling me that I needed to get back home *immediately* was all too fucking much.

"It's not because I don't love you. I do. I've never felt this way about anyone, ever. But..." I sighed and knew I needed to give him *something*. "My mom is sick."

"What do you mean sick?"

"She doesn't want anyone to know," I continued. "I can't go into it. I'm probably not coming back to school. She needs me with her."

"That doesn't mean that we can't still, you know, be together."

"I'm *home*, Devin. That's like a two-hour plane ride. I can't do that to you. I can't put that much space between us and expect to be able to maintain a relationship."

"I can live without sex, Patrick. I'd settle for hearing your voice on the phone. I can come see you over break. We can make it work. People a whole continent apart make relationships work."

I shook my head. "No."

"You can't just say no to me and expect me to accept it, Patrick. I love you, goddamn it." He punched me in the chest. It hurt, but not as much as seeing him trying so hard not to cry. Not as much as it hurt to hold in my own emotions. Trying so damn hard not to let him see how much this was hurting me too.

I rubbed my chest. "I know."

"You want me to let you leave and never see you again?"

"I never said that."

"That's what you're implying."

"Devin, I'm not doing this because I want to."

"Then why are you doing it?"

"Because I need to."

"Fuck you." He punched me the chest again. This one issued a grunt from me.

"You can hit me all you want. I probably deserve it," I said.

"You're not even worth it." He shoved past me and slammed the door behind him. I squeezed my eyes closed and leaned back against it. I gave myself two minutes to cry it out. Then, I had a plane to catch.

After that, I went home and helped take care of my mom. That was part of how I found myself in a New York hotel, sleeping with an actor with the most beautiful eyes I'd ever seen on a man.

I slipped through the quiet halls of the hotel. I hated that Devin had popped into my head when I was with Josh. I had managed to shove him to the back of my head since I had left campus. I hadn't even gone back to pack up my room. I had sent one of my Mom's assistants to pack up and check out of my room for me, like I had been too much of a pansy to take the chance of seeing him again.

What bothered me most though, was the fact that he hadn't even tried to contact me. Although, I hadn't exactly tried either. Now school had let out two weeks before and I wasn't sure how to get a hold of him. Sure, I could e-mail him. I could call his cell phone. I could probably even look up his home address in the campus directory.

I was just pulling my clothes back off to hop into the shower when my phone started to ring. I took the time to answer it.

"Hi, Mom," I said. "—No, I'm fine. It's just kind of late. What's going on?" I waited for her reply while I sat down on the couch. Her voice was kind of soft and she said she'd only wanted to talk. "Mom, you're in the hospital. You should be getting your sleep."

"Pssht," she scoffed. "Don't talk to me like I'm a kid, Patrick."

"Ma," I yawned, "it's like what? Three in the morning? I'm barely awake."

"Oh yeah... What are you doing answering your phone? I didn't really expect you to answer."

"I just got in."

"Ooh, fun night out? Who's the girl? It's not that snotty bitch they have playing my side-kick female, is it?"

"I had a couple of drinks with the guys."

"Ooh," she repeated, "is my cute little boy finally taking after his mother?"

"Ma!"

"It's okay, you know I don't really care. Just so long as you don't introduce me to your boyfriends. You know how I get. That's why I sent you to the set in my place. I probably would have passed out with all those boys fawning over me."

"You're not full of yourself at all."

"Hmm. Well, I'll let you sleep. I'll see you tomorrow."

"Yeah," I confirmed. "G'night Mom. Don't stay up watching Logo all night. You need to get some sleep."

"I will," she scoffed. "Besides, this late it's just re-runs of Drag Race and I've already seen every season a dozen times."

I laughed, shaking my head before I hung up. I shut my phone off, tossing it down on the coffee table before I stood again. The hot water in the shower felt good and I was relieved to finally crawl into bed.

The next afternoon, I pressed a kiss to Mom's forehead. She looked pretty good for a woman in a hospital. She was up and moving around, sitting on the end of the bed rather than laying in it.

"Hey. How are you?"

"I'm okay. I'll be glad to get out of here."

"When do they think you can leave?"

"Probably a couple of more days. They want to make sure everything is normal."

"Well, you should rest."

"Tell me about the movie. Are they slaughtering it?"

"Ma, I wouldn't know the difference if they did. It looks like it's going well."

"I don't like that Josh kid. He doesn't fit my character at all," she sighed.

I shrugged.

"He's the one that's gay, right? Make sure he keeps a distance at the premier."

"You know, you should really work on your people skills. You miss a lot of great opportunities."

"It's not like it's all gay men!" She scoffed. "Just the cute ones..."

"You'd like what they're doing. I was told that, while they can't be a graphic as you are, they're doing their best to make it as true to the book as possible."

"Good." She nodded approvingly.

We both looked up as a spunky looking girl walked in, wearing a pencil skirt and a low cut top.

"Patrick, welcome home!" She came over to kiss me rather bluntly on the lips. "How was New York?"

"Fine," I replied. "How have things been going here, Mattie?"

Mattie was my mom's assistant –one of three. She had become a close friend over the last couple of years and Mom really depended on her for stability.

"Good," she answered. "Doctors said your mom can probably go home at the end of the week."

"That's great."

"Unfortunately, she's also on three new medications." Mattie pulled a brush out from one of the travel bags along the wall. I watched as they moved so Mattie could sit behind Mom to start brushing her hair. "They're just precautionary for a couple of weeks."

Mom sighed. "I wish everyone would believe me when I say I'm fine."

"You're fine because you're taking meds." Mattie paused looking up at me. "Oh yeah, there was a guy who stopped by the house looking for you."

"Looking for me?" I raised an eyebrow. "What for?"

"I don't know. He said he was a friend from school and that he'd come back."

"Did he say who he was?"

"No." She shook her head. "He kind of booked it out of there before I could ask."

"What'd he look like?"

"Umm...tall, dark hair, had a motorcycle. I dunno. Kinda cute, if you're into that."

I thought for a moment. I had no idea who it could possibly be. I had few 'friends' while I was at school. Most that would call themselves my 'friends' were girls I used for sexual gratification. I didn't have anyone that I was close to...

"Whatever," I shrugged, "I'm not going to worry about it just now."

"Honey, if you've got a friend waiting for you, you should go."

"Ma, if it's a friend, they know how to call me."

She hummed, and picked up the remote for the television. "I was watching Logo last night—"

"Before or after you called me?" I raised an eyebrow.

"Before," she rolled her eyes. "As was saying, they had this excellent movie on, but I missed like the first half of it. What I don't understand though is, why does everything 'gay' have to have this low budget feel to it? Or is that just me?"

"Just visuals," Mattie replied. "Your books aren't like that."

"Meh," Mom scoffed, "I beg to differ."

Mattie looked to me for help, but I shrugged. "I haven't read one, so I can't really argue."

Mom turned to look at me. "Why is that?"

"Mom, you write gay erotica. First, it's *gay erotica*. Second, you're my mother!"

"So? Not *everything* I write is embarrassing." She rolled her eyes. "A few of my books hardly have any sex in them at all."

"I don't really feel like having this conversation, thanks."

We were quiet for a few minutes. Mattie kept brushing Mom's hair before braiding it, and Mom was enthralled with a variety show. I watched the two of them and was pretty sure that if my mom were a lesbian, and Mattie didn't have a girlfriend, they would make a really cute couple. I jumped when Mom suddenly clapped her hand over her mouth and shouted, "Oh my god!"

"What?" I pressed my hand to my heart, like that would help slow it back down from the jolt.

"I need you to go home and get me the green notebook that's sitting on my desk. The purple one too."

"What for?"

"Because I've got six stories to finish writing before I die, silly."

"Mom!"

"Well, I do! I put away the Royal Night story because I was stuck, but I just got a fantastic idea. So hurry up and go get it before I forget what I was thinking!"

"Patrick, just go get it for her," Mattie chided. "Sam, write the idea down so you don't forget." She got up and pushed a yellow legal pad and pen into Mom's hands.

I sighed, getting up and stretching my arms over my head. "Can you write on that for now? I'd like to get some sleep. I had an early flight. I'll bring your laptop for you too."

"Yeah, I suppose." Mom dismissed me. I should have felt slighted, but I knew she was just excited to have some creative juices going again. She stopped me before I exited, "Wait –what was Ron's brother's name... It started with a D?"

"David?" Mattie guessed.

"No..."

"Derek?"

"I don't think that's it."

Mom talked about her characters like they were her kids. Even though I didn't read her stories, I still knew the characters like they were my siblings. "Devin, wasn't it?"

"Yes!"

It wasn't until I was out in my car that the thought struck me about who had appeared at my doorstep while I was gone.

I was woken up when the doorbell rang. I was tempted to ignore it, but knowing my luck it was important. I pulled on a clean pair of jeans from my drawer and made my way downstairs. I was just zipping them up when I cracked open the door after another insistent bell toll.

"Yeah?" My eyes were kind of blurry from being sleep deprived.

"Patrick?"

I squeezed my eyes closed, trying to focus before looking up, "Devin..."

"Hi."

He looked good. Well, better then good. My jeans felt constrictive, and I had only just laid eyes on the guy. His hair was different. More styled. Shorter. He was wearing a light leather jacket and tight jeans. I could see a bright red motorcycle in the drive.

"What are you doing here?" I asked.

"I wanted...needed to see you."

"Why didn't you call me?"

"I wasn't sure if you'd answer if you saw that it was me," he admitted.

We were quiet. I wasn't sure what he wanted me to say. I didn't have anything. All I could think about was pulling him inside and doing him on the entry way carpet.

"You didn't come back to school," he finally continued.

"No, I didn't."

"Some girl came and packed up all of your stuff, but she didn't get your art back from your professors. I managed to talk them into giving it to me. I have it. I can mail it."

"It isn't that big of a deal."

He blushed, looking down at the ground. He scuffed the toe of his boot against the concrete step. "I'm sorry. I shouldn't have come here."

"You should have called me first," I corrected. Fuck, he was here. Standing in front of me. The painful relief of laying eyes on him again was... Complicated. "Now isn't the best time."

"Your Mom?" He guessed.

"Mom is fine," I assured him. "Or, she will be for now. I had an early flight this morning."

He nodded. "Right. I'm sorry. I'll just go."

"No, wait..." I couldn't stop myself from pulling him back. I felt like electricity was running up my arm as I grabbed his hand. "Come in. You came all this way. Let me get dressed."

"You're tired. It's fine."

"Devin," I pulled him closer. "Come in. Please?"

He looked up at me before he nodded. "Okay."

I closed the door behind us and watched him look around.

"This place is really big."

"Yeah, I guess."

"Did you guys always live here?"

"We moved in here five years ago. Before, we lived in a place across town that was about a third this size."

"So...where's your room?"

"Always straight to the point with you." I let out a laugh, reassured that he hadn't changed.

He blushed. "I didn't imply that I wanted— "

"You're right you didn't," I admitted. I walked towards the stairs. "It's this way."

He followed behind me, looking at the walls. They were littered with pictures of Mom and me. Of people that had come in and out of our lives over the years. There were a couple of award certificates hung up sporadically too. The ones Mom wasn't totally ashamed of at any rate. Maybe shame wasn't the right emotion she felt for some of her awards...more like mortification due to the attention.

"So, this it?" He sat down on my bed, looking around.

"Yeah." I pulled on a plain t-shirt from my closet. "It's not as exciting as the rest of the house. I haven't used it much since leaving for school."

"I came by earlier. Some girl answered the door."

"That would have been Mattie. She's my mom's assistant."

"She said you were in New York."

"Mom wanted me to check on some things with the new movie."

He nodded, "Oh. So, you were rubbing elbows with the likes of Josh Capernelli and David Chambers, huh?"

"I met them, yes."

"Should I be jealous?"

"Well, we broke up, so...no."

A flush rose in his cheeks. "Right."

"How long are you I town for?"

"As long as you'll have me." He looked totally innocent as he said it. I wanted to take him into my arms and kiss him...but I resisted.

I came over to the bed and stood between his knees. "Why didn't you call me? I told you I couldn't be your boyfriend. I never said I didn't want to talk to you again."

"It was hard," he admitted. "Months later, I still think about you every single day. I tried dating other guys but I can't force myself to feel the same way about them as I do about you."

"That's flattering."

"What about you," he asked, leaning up. He looped his fingers into my belt loops, looking up at me. "Girlfriend?"

I shook my head. "Haven't had time for a girlfriend."

"Boyfriend?"

"No boyfriends."

"Fuck buddy?"

"If you're asking if I had sex, Devin, yes, I had sex. I had sex last night if you really need to know." I tried to ignore that hurt look on his face. I tilted his chin back up to look him in the eye. "But it was sex with someone who didn't matter. It wasn't the same as it was with you."

"And sex with me did matter?"

"Of course, it did. I fucking love you." I had to kiss him. It had been so long since I tasted that familiar lemony flavor of his mouth. He bit his lip as I pulled away.

"You left me, without even explaining anything." His voice wasn't accusing. Just sad.

"I had to," I said. "It was like, if I stayed and tried to explain everything, I wouldn't have been able to rationalize with myself why I had to leave."

"Why did you leave?"

"I told you. My mom is sick."

"She has people other than you to take care of her," he insisted. "She'd want you to be with someone who makes you happy, Patrick."

"Devin, it's not that simple. It's been just me and my mom since...forever. I have to be here with her."

"But she's doing better now, right?"

"For now."

"Are you coming back to school?"

"Probably not. Not for next semester anyway."

"I want to be with you."

I didn't know what to say to that. I pulled my fingers through his hair, liking the softness of it. I wanted to be with him too, but that would be really hard to explain to everyone... A legitimately straight man who liked nothing better than squeeze a pair of boobs in his hands or watching a feminine mouth work over his cock, was taking a pure thrill out of fucking and being fucked by a very hot specimen of manhood... It was bizarre.

"Say something," he urged. I started to try to kiss him, but he stopped me. "No, I need you to *say something* to me. What's happening here?"

"I want to fuck you," I declared. "I don't know what we are. Where we stand. What the hell we're doing here...but I know I want to fuck you. Only you."

"Only me, or only me as far as men go?"

"Does it matter? I don't see any women around."

"Yeah, it does."

"You're the only person I want to have sex with this badly, Devin." I forced his hands away so I could kiss him. "It's been a while. I'm not really sure what I'm doing anymore. Last night proved that for me."

"So, you really did have sex last night? You weren't just saying that to make me mad?"

"I did. It was...okay."

"Just okay?"

"Yeah. I mean, it had a lot of build up to it. When we actually doing it, the whole time I was just thinking *what's going on? Why am I doing this*?"

"Who were you with?"

"You don't want to know that."

"I do," he insisted.

"No, you don't. You'll just get jealous and then you won't sleep with me."

"Probably."

"Fuck me first," I tempted him. "If you renew my faith in my abilities, I'll tell you."

"Or you could tell me now,and if I'm not made totally jealous, I'll let you fuck me instead?"

"You got that itch to be on the bottom again, huh?"

"I always have that itch."

I licked my lips and let out a soft sigh. Then I came clean. "I had a few drinks with the guys from the cast. I went back to the hotel with Josh Capernelli. He was...he was okay. I thought he was cute. But he wasn't you."

"Did you give him that whole 'I'm straight' spiel?"

I smiled. "Yeah."

"I'm sorry to break it to you, but I'm not going to get jealous over some Hollywood heartthrob." He rolled his eyes. "Hell, I'd probably do Josh Capernelli too. He's got a nice ass."

I laughed, shaking my head. "So...we're okay?"

"Yeah, I guess. That was your one free celebrity pass, Patrick."

I grinned and kissed him again. I pushed him back into my bed. I got up on the edge, bringing my hands under his butt to pull him higher on the mattress underneath me. I loved the big queen-sized bed already. We had much more room to move around then we ever did back in the dorms. I couldn't get enough of him as I brought my arms around him, pressing close. Our arms and legs ended up in a tangle and he pushed over top of me.

"You got supplies?"

"Ah, fuck." I sighed. "I don't know. Let me check." I kissed him before pushing him off me again. He watched me cross the room, pulling off my shirt after digging through my bed side table. Nothing.

"I'm gonna go look in the bathroom. Get naked while I'm gone."

I made my way quickly as I could towards the bathroom. I was lucky enough to come across a bottle of lube that I didn't remember purchasing and wasn't going to ask questions about who else would have bought it and for what purpose. I was just thankful that it was there. It took another minute before I found a box of condoms I must have stashed before leaving for school. A peek at the expiration date had me breathing a sigh of relief.

"I found some." I tossed the supplies across the room towards the bed before wiggling out of my jeans. I took my time, edging onto the bed. I was pleased to see that he had listened to me about the 'get naked' bit.

"Excellent." He wrapped his arms around my neck, kissing me again. I didn't want to take my lips away from his. He felt so good against me. His hands felt silky smooth as they trailed down my back.

"Hmm, you haven't shaved in a while." I grinned, running my palm over his pliant cock.

"know you don't like the bald look... But I couldn't stop shaving my balls, I'm sorry."

"That's okay." I laughed. I slid down his body to lick him. "It makes it easier to suck on them."

He groaned, biting his lip, "And you claim you're straight..."

"I'm queer as hell when I'm with you," I teased. It felt nice to say it out loud. Maybe eventually I'd be able to admit I was queer even when he *wasn't* around. I loved the way he felt in my mouth. I loved the little noise he made in the back of his throat as I ran my tongue down his entire length before taking him into my mouth. He reached down to pull gently on my hair. I wanted my mouth to be everywhere, taking him in.

"You feel so good..." He sat up, hugging my shoulders. I looked up and he kissed me. "I missed you so much. You have no idea at all."

"I think I can imagine," I admitted. I slid back up to straddle his hips between my knees. "I missed you too."

"Are you just going to tease me, or are you going to fuck me?" He teased. He opened the bottle of lube with a cracking sound and I moaned, flinching a little as the cool liquid fell along our lengths. His hands wrapped around both of us, rubbing them together and coating our warm pricks with the lube. I closed my eyes, pressing my face into his shoulder. I kissed his neck, sucking his skin between my teeth. He groaned, stroking me harder. I always had a little bit of a weakness for frottage...

"I need you to fuck me," he hummed. He bit on my ear which incited another groan.

I spun him around, pushing him down over the foot of the bed. He caught himself with his hands as I knelt down behind him, licking his opening. He gasped, and grabbed for the lube and the condom box, pushing them towards me.

"We can do that stuff later. I need you now."

I hummed, giving his puckered hole a kiss before liberally applying lube to his backside. I stroked my fingers inside of him, making him moan. Unlike in our dorm rooms, neither of us were having any qualms about making noise –there was no one else to hear us. And he moaned so well...

"Fuck me," he growled, looking at me over his shoulder.

I wiped my lubricated hand on the bedspread before taking a minute to roll on the condom. I positioned myself quickly and slid in with surprising ease. Devin moaned even louder.

"Ahh, you feel so good!" He put his hands on my hips and slowly straightened so we were standing front-to-back. His hands came up and stroked my face. My skin prickled as his fingertips brushed the start of my five o'clock shadow. My arms wrapped around his waist, and I just pushed softly into him. "How did I go so long without you?"

"I don't know." I kissed his neck. I turned his face to kiss him before forcing my tongue into his mouth. His tongue dueled with mine for a few moments before he sighed contentedly.

"Okay, you need to move," he grinned, leaning back against me. He reached, touching the back of my neck as I started to thrust into him. "Faster than that. I'm not made of porcelain."

"Really? 'Cause you're kind of pale and fragile looking," I teased.

"Fuck me as hard as you can," he requested.

"I don't want to hurt you," I whispered. "Besides, it's kind of hard when we're standing."

"Then I'll do it." He moved his hips forward and then thrust back. The jerk made me tip just a little and I grabbed his hips again to stay steady.

"Bend back over and I'll do it." I kissed his cheek. "Then I'll flip you over and it do it that way. Then we can do it on our sides and any other which way you want."

He grinned, biting his tongue between his teeth. He looked so damn cute. I had the fleeting thought of maybe not being able to be able to hold on in this position long enough to try anything else. He obeyed me quietly though, leaning up on his arms and wiggling his butt at me. I wiped my hands off again before grabbing his hips. I started out slow, like I had been, but a disgruntled noise from his throat made me move a little faster.

"C'mon Patrick..." he moaned. "Pound into me..."

"Since when are you such a masochist?"

"I'm not," he sighed. "I just really need to feel that you're here with me..."

"You don't feel like that now?" I leaned forward to kiss the back of his shoulder before I nodded. "Okay...but if I hurt you, you tell me! Don't hold it in."

It took me a few seconds to stamp down my apprehension, but I did, and it wasn't a whole lot longer before I was pounding into him as hard and fast as I could. I listened to his moaning and groaning for notes of distress, but never heard any "no" or "stop", so I kept going.

"Ah-ah—ah..." he panted loudly, "fuck me, fuck me, fuck me..."

I grinned. "You have such a dirty mouth." I paused to push him further up onto the bed. I knelt behind him and pressed my palms into the bed on either side of him. Laying over top of him, I couldn't push quite as deep, but that was OK. I bucked my hips against him, and he panted some more.

"I think I'm gonna come!"

"I haven't even touched you!"

"Then flip me over and do it!"

I stepped away from him just long enough to do as he said. He grabbed a pillow to shove under his hips, and I pushed back into him. He tipped his head back, moaning. I kissed his wrists as his hands pressed onto my shoulders. I devoured his mouth, wrapping a hand around him. He let out a cry—a mixture of excitement and arousal. I kissed his chin and then his throat. The source of all those great noises he was making.

He arched forward as he came, wrapping his arms around my waist. He tightened around me. I lost myself too when I saw the pure ecstasy on his face. He gasped, laying back, still kind of twitching. I groaned, letting him take over stroking himself while I pulled out, stroking myself; making sure everything emptied into the condom before pulling it off to dispose of it in the trash.

I slid off to his side, nuzzling his cheek. I couldn't help but reach down between his legs and stroke a finger inside of his still-loose hole. He moaned, turning to kiss me roughly.

"You're gonna make me hard again..."

"Ahh, I think we're done for at least an hour or two," I groaned. "If you can get me up again, I'll fuck you."

He sighed, turning onto his side and pulled me close. He moaned at the adjustment, my fingers still probing inside of him. He wrapped his arms around my shoulders and kissed me.

"Patrick?"

"Devin."

"Will you promise me something?"

"Is this the sex talking?"

"No," he hit me in the shoulder, "I'm being serious."

I nodded. "Okay, what's up?"

"Promise me you'll never leave me like that again." He shook his head. "I mean, if it comes down to it, you can leave me of course. But give me some closure, okay? Don't just leave without explaining anything. Like what we have doesn't matter."

"I don't plan on leaving you, ever again. I missed you so fucking much. I'm so sorry. For everything." I wrapped my arms around him, pressing face into his neck. It took him a second, but his arms wrapped around me too. He felt so good in my arms. Better than any girl I'd ever had sex with, and much better than any guy. I suddenly felt kind of sleepy.

"You fallin' asleep on me, Patrick?" He stroked his fingertips through my hair. I nodded, releasing a sigh. "Go to sleep then." His lips brushed my cheek.

"You gonna stay here with me?" I asked.

"I told you before, I'll stay as long as you want me to."

"Good."

I felt his arms tighten around me. For the first time in awhile, I felt safe in someone else's arms as I fell asleep. ...I'd worry about how I was going to introduce him to my mom when we woke up.

Don't miss out!

Visit the website below and you can sign up to receive emails whenever Sam LaRose publishes a new book. There's no charge and no obligation.

https://books2read.com/r/B-A-YMEK-THFFB

Connecting independent readers to independent writers.

Did you love *Freedom to Choose*? Then you should read *Light The Lamp*[1] by Sam LaRose!

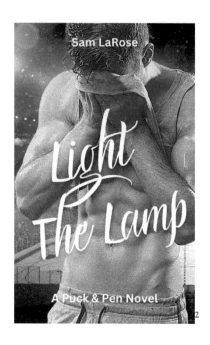

"Where do your ideas come from then?"

"I don't know. It's this nagging inkling of what-if."

"I understand this nagging feeling." The man took a step closer. "Like, this voice in my head that keeps telling me to kiss you."

Harper's eyes widened slightly. "What? Why?"

"Why?" He sounded surprised. "Why not? You are sexiest person in this bar. You stood out to me right away."

---

1. https://books2read.com/u/3yWMr6

2. https://books2read.com/u/3yWMr6

Pieter Ivanov is skating into his 10th pro-hockey season with a new team, in a new city. Fresh off a successful play-off run, he's looking forward to connecting with his teammates and settling in. When he joins his captain for drinks, he doesn't expect the night to change his life.

Harper Wyatt has lived in Manhattan for nearly a decade. As a still-floundering author, they take the little wins where they can and their favorite place to do that is the Mounting Bison. Celebrating the publication of their second book with their besties, they anticipate a couple of drinks, lots of laughs, and then calling it an early night.

When Pietr spies Harper across the bar, he's immediately smitten. He has no idea what "non-binary" means, but he's open minded and willing to learn. Harper typically steers clear of the Osprey players that frequent the bar with their captain, but Pietr has zero qualms about approaching them –in the bar bathroom of all places. And thus, in the first Meet Cute of their life, Harper's quiet, single life is upended.

This slice-of-life romance is sure to thrill romance readers looking for diverse representation and a unique story with cozy vibes. Fans of the Dark Little Town series will love the connections to a New York they've grown familiar with. Light the Lamp features multiple LGBTQ+ characters, alternative relationship structures, and a lot of spice.

Read more at www.samlarose.com.

Also by Sam LaRose

Dark Little Town
Real Talk
Pants Optional
Something More

Dylan Duology
Honest Lies
Press Play

Puck & Pen
Light The Lamp

Standalone
Freedom to Choose

Watch for more at www.samlarose.com.

About the Author

Sam is a nonbinary person in rural Wisconsin. They work as a libary director and live in an old farm house with too many cats and a rabbit.

Read more at www.samlarose.com.

Milton Keynes UK
Ingram Content Group UK Ltd.
UKHW010714040923
428018UK00014B/805